D1377745

Community Helpers

Story Time with Our Librarian

Bonnie Phelps

illustrated by
Anita Morra

PowerKiDS
press.

New York

Published in 2017 by The Rosen Publishing Group, Inc.
29 East 21st Street, New York, NY 10010

First Edition

Managing Editor: Nathalie Beullens-Maoui
Editor: Caitie McAneney
Book Design: Michael Flynn
Illustrator: Anita Morra

Cataloging-in-Publication Data

Names: Phelps, Bonnie.
Title: Story time with our librarian / Bonnie Phelps.
Description: New York : PowerKids Press, 2017. | Series: Community helpers | Includes index.
Identifiers: ISBN 9781499427080 (pbk.) | ISBN 9781499430349 (library bound) | ISBN 9781499427097 (6 pack)
Subjects: LCSH: Librarians–Juvenile literature. | Libraries–Juvenile literature.
Classification: LCC Z682.P54 2017 | DDC 020.92–dc23

Manufactured in the United States of America

CPSIA Compliance Information: Batch #BW17PK: For Further Information contact Rosen Publishing, New York, New York at 1-800-237-9932

Contents

My mom and I walk to the library. It's story time!

I love listening to our librarian read.

He lets me pick the book today.

I pick a book about pirates.

I sit with my friends to listen.

The librarian is a good reader.
He makes funny voices!

My friend Mario picks
the next book. It's
about ballerinas.

The librarian points to the
pictures in the book.

This helps me follow
the story.

The librarian shows us his favorite book.

It's about sea animals.

I learn a lot from listening.

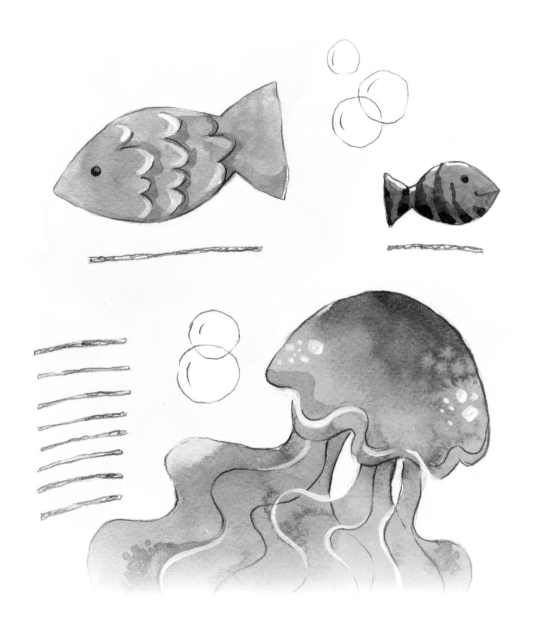

I see pictures of whales and fish.

The librarian shows us where we can
pick our own books.

I pick two to bring home.

The librarian knows so much about books.

He helps everyone find the book they want!

Words to Know

ballerina

book

pirate

Index